UNDER THE WINDOW

BY
KATE GREENAWAY

This edition is distributed by
AVENEL BOOKS
a division of Crown Publishers, Inc.

CONTENTS

UNDER the window is my garden,
   Where sweet, sweet flowers grow;
And in the pear-tree dwells a robin,
   The dearest bird I know.

Tho' I peep out betimes in the morning,
   Still the flowers are up the first;
Then I try and talk to the robin,
   And perhaps he'd chat—if he durst.

KC

WILL you be my little wife,
  If I ask you? Do!
I'll buy you such a Sunday frock,
  A nice umbrella, too.

And you shall have a little hat,
  With such a long white feather,
A pair of gloves, and sandal shoes,
  The softest kind of leather.

And you shall have a tiny house,
  A beehive full of bees,
A little cow, a largish cat,
  And green sage cheese.

K G

14

You see, merry Phillis, that dear little maid,
 Has invited Belinda to tea;
Her nice little garden is shaded by trees—
 What pleasanter place could there be?

There's a cake full of plums, there are strawberries too,
 And the table is set on the green;
I'm fond of a carpet all daisies and grass—
 Could a prettier picture be seen?

A blackbird (yes, blackbirds delight in warm weather,)
 Is flitting from yonder high spray;
He sees the two little ones talking together—
 No wonder the blackbird is gay!

15

THREE tabbies took out their cats to tea,
As well-behaved tabbies as well could be:
Each sat in the chair that each preferred,
They mewed for their milk, and they sipped and purred.
Now tell me this (as these cats you've seen them)—
How many lives had these cats between them?

LITTLE Fanny wears a hat
  Like her ancient Grannie;
Tommy's hoop was (think of that!)
  Given him by Fanny.

"MARGERY BROWN, on the top of the hill,
Why are you standing, idle still?"
"Oh, I'm looking over to London town;
Shall I see the horsemen if I go down?"

"Margery Brown, on the top of the hill,
Why are you standing, listening still?"
"Oh, I hear the bells of London ring,
And I hear the men and the maidens sing."

"Margery Brown, on the top of the hill,
Why are you standing, waiting still?"
"Oh, a knight is there, but I can't go down,
For the bells ring strangely in London town."

Little wind, blow on the hill-top,
  Little wind, blow down the plain;
Little wind, blow up the sunshine,
  Little wind, blow off the rain.

INDEED it is true, it is perfectly true;
Believe me, indeed, I am playing no tricks;
An old man and his dog bide up there in the moon,
And he's cross as a bundle of sticks.

KG.

School is over,
  Oh, what fun!
Lessons finished,
  Play begun.

Who'll run fastest,
  You or I?
Who'll laugh loudest?
  Let us try.

K.G.

"LITTLE Polly, will you go a-walking to-day?"
"Indeed, little Susan, I will, if I may."
"Little Polly, your mother has said you may go;
She was nice to say 'Yes;' she should never say 'No.'"

"A rook has a nest on the top of the tree—
A big ship is coming from over the sea:
Now, which would be nicest, the ship or the nest?"
"Why, that would be nicest that Polly likes best."

As I was walking up the street,
　The steeple bells were ringing;
As I sat down at Mary's feet,
　The sweet, sweet birds were singing.

As I walked far into the world,
　I met a little fairy;
She plucked this flower, and, as it's sweet,
　I've brought it home to Mary.

FIVE little sisters walking in a row;
Now, isn't that the best way for little girls to go?
Each had a round hat, each had a muff,
And each had a new pelisse of soft green stuff.

Five little marigolds standing in a row;
Now, isn't that the best way for marigolds to grow?
Each with a green stalk, and all the five had got
A bright yellow flower, and a new red pot.

In go-cart so tiny
   My sister I drew;
And I've promised to draw her
   The wide world through.

We have not yet started—
   I own it with sorrow—
Because our trip's always
   Put off till to-morrow.

SOME geese went out a-walking,
    To breakfast and to dine;
They craned their necks, and plumed themselves—
    They numbered four from nine;
With their cackle, cackle, cackle!
    They thought themselves so fine.

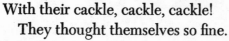

A dame went walking by herself,
    A very ancient crone;
She, said. "I wish that all you geese
    Were starved to skin and bone!
Do stop that cackle, cackle, now,
    And leave me here alone."

You are going out to tea to-day,
  So mind how you behave;
Let all accounts I have of you
  Be pleasant ones, I crave.

Don't spill your tea, or gnaw your bread,
  And don't tease one another;
And Tommy mustn't talk too much,
  Or quarrel with his brother.

Say "If you please," and "Thank you, Nurse:"
    Come home at eight o'clock;
And, Fanny, pray be careful that
    You do not tear your frock.

Now, mind your manners, children five.
    Attend to what I say;
And then, perhaps, I'll let you go
    Again another day.

Poor Dicky's dead!—The bell we toll,
And lay him in the deep, dark hole.
The sun may shine, the clouds may rain,
But Dick will never pipe again!
His quilt will be as sweet as ours—
Bright buttercups and cuckoo flowers.

UP you go, shuttlecocks, ever so high!
Why come you down again, shuttlecocks—why?
When you have got so far, why do you fall?
Where all are high, which is highest of all?

K.G

Tommy was a silly boy,
  "I can fly," he said;
He started off, but very soon,
  He tumbled on his head.

His little sister Prue was there,
  To see how he would do it;
She knew that, after all his boast,
  Full dearly Tom would rue it!

HIGGLEDY, piggledy! see how they run!
Hopperty, popperty! what is the fun?
Has the sun or the moon tumbled into the sea?
What is the matter, now? Pray tell it me!

Higgledy, piggledy! how can I tell?
Hopperty, popperty! hark to the bell!
The rats and the mice even scamper away;
Who can say what may not happen to-day?

WHICH is the way to Somewhere Town?
　　Oh, up in the morning early;
Over the tiles and the chimney-pots,
　　That is the way, quite clearly.

And which is the door to Somewhere Town?
　　Oh, up in the morning early;
The round red sun is the door to go through.
　　That is the way, quite clearly.

The boat sails away, like a bird on the wing,
And the little boys dance on the sands in a ring.
The wind may fall, or the wind may rise—
You are foolish to go; you will stay if you're wise.
The little boys dance, and the little girls run:
If it's bad to have money, it's worse to have none.

35

Pipe thee high, and pipe thee low,
Let the little feet go faster;
Blow your penny trumpet—blow!
Well done, little master!

POLLY's, Peg's, and Poppety's
  Mamma was kind and good;
She gave them each, one happy day,
  A little scarf and hood.

A bonnet for each girl she bought,
  To shield them from the sun;
They wore them in the snow and rain,
  And thought it mighty fun.

But sometimes there were naughty boys,
  Who called to them at play,
And made this rude remark—"My eye!
  Three Grannies out to-day!"

Bowl away! bowl away!
  Fast as you can;
He who can fastest bowl,
  He is my man!
Up and down, round about,—
  Don't let it fall;
Ten times, or twenty times,
  Beat, beat them all!

"For what are you longing, you three little boys?
    Oh, what would you like to eat?"
"We should like some apples, or gingerbread—
    Or a fine big drum to beat."

"Oh, what will you give me, you three little boys,
    In exchange for these good, good things?"
"Some bread and cheese, and some radishes,
    And our little brown bird that sings."

"Now, that won't do, you three little chums,
    I'll have something better than that—
Two of your fingers, and two of your thumbs,
    In the crown of your largest hat!"

KC

O RING the bells! O ring the bells!
　We bid you, sirs, good morning;
Give thanks, we pray—our flowers are gay,
　And fair for your adorning.

O ring the bells! O ring the bells!
　Good sirs, accept our greeting;
Where we have been, the woods are green.
　So, hey! for our next meeting.

Then ring the bells! then ring the bells!
　　For this fair time of Maying;
Our blooms we bring, and while we sing,
　　O! hark to what we're saying.

O ring the bells! O ring the bells!
　　We'll sing a song with any;
And may each year bring *you* good cheer,
　　And each of *us* a penny.

I saw a ship that sailed the sea,
   It left me as the sun went down;
The white birds flew, and followed it
   To town—to London town.

Right sad were we to stand alone,
   And see it pass so far away;
And yet we knew some ship would come—
   Some other ship—some other day.

Yes, that's the girl that struts about,
    She's very proud,—so very proud!
Her *bow-wow*'s quite as proud as she:
They both are very wrong to be
    So proud—so very proud.

See, Jane and Willy laugh at her,
    They say she's very proud!
Says Jane, "My stars!—they're very silly;"
"Indeed they are," cries little Willy,
    "To walk so stiff and proud."

It was Tommy who said,
    "The sweet spring-time is come;
I see the birds flit,
    And I hear the bees hum.

"Oho! Mister Lark,
    Up aloft in the sky,
Now, which is the happiest—
    Is it you, sir, or I?"

"SHALL I sing?" says the Lark,
  "Shall I bloom?" says the Flower:
"Shall I come?" says the Sun,
  "Or shall I?" says the Shower.

Sing your song, pretty Bird,
  Roses, bloom for an hour;
Shine on, dearest Sun,
  Go away, naughty Shower!

Little Miss Patty and Master Paul
Have found two snails on the garden wall.
"These snails," said Paul, "how slow they walk!
A great deal slower than we can talk.
Make haste, Mr. Snail, travel quicker, I pray;
In a race with our tongues you'd be beaten to-day."

Yes, it is sad of them—
    Shocking to me;
Bad—yes, it's bad of them—
    Bad of all three.

Warnings they've had from me.
    Still I repeat them—
Cold is the water—the
    Fishes will eat them.
Yet they will row about,

    Tho' I say "Fie!" to them;
Fathers may scold at it,
    Mothers may cry to them.

Now, all of you, give heed unto
   The tale I now relate,
About two girls and one small boy,
   A cat, and a green gate.

*   *   *   *   *

Alack! since I began to speak
   (And what I say is true),
It's all gone out of my poor head—
   And so good-bye to you!

WHAT is Tommy running for
  Running for,
  Running for?
What is Tommy running for,
  On this fine day?

Jimmy will run after Tommy,
  After Tommy,
  After Tommy;
That's what Tommy's running for,
  On this fine day.

A BUTCHER's boy met a baker's boy
  (It was all of a summer day);
Said the butcher's boy to the baker's boy,
  "Will you please to walk my way?"

Said the butcher's boy to the baker's boy,
  "My trade's the best in town,"
"If you dare say that," said the baker's boy,
  "I shall have to knock you down!"

Said the butcher's boy to the baker's boy,
  "That's a wicked thing to do;
And I think, before you've knocked me down,
  The cook will blow up *you!*"

The twelve Miss Pelicoes,
    Of course, to school were sent;
Their parents wished them to excel
    In each accomplishment.

The twelve Miss Pelicoes
    Played music—*Fal-lal-la!*
Which consequently made them all
    The pride of their papa.

The twelve Miss Pelicoes
    Learnt dancing and the globes;
Which proves that they were wise, and had
    That patience which was Job's.

K.C

THE twelve Miss Pelicoes
   Were twelve sweet little girls;
Some wore their hair in pigtail plaits,
   And some of them wore curls.

The twelve Miss Pelicoes
   Had dinner every day;—
A not uncommon thing at all,
   You probably will say.

The twelve Miss Pelicoes
   Went sometimes for a walk;
It also is a well-known fact
   That all of them could talk.

The twelve Miss Pelicoes
   Were always most polite—
Said "If you please," and "Many thanks,"
   "Good morning," and "Good night."

The twelve Miss Pelicoes
   You plainly see, were taught
To do the things they didn't like,
   Which means, the things they ought.

Now, fare ye well, Miss Pelicoes,
   I wish ye a good day;—
About these twelve Miss Pelicoes
   I've nothing more to say.

LITTLE baby, if I threw
This fair blossom down to you,
Would you catch it as you stand,
Holding up each tiny hand,
Looking out of those grey eyes,
Where such deep, deep wonder lies?

THE finest, biggest fish, you see,
Will be the trout that's caught by me.
But if the monster will not bite,
Why, then I'll hook a little mite.

PRINCE FINIKIN and his mamma
  Sat sipping their bohea;
"Good gracious!" said his Highness, "why,
  What girl is this I see?

"Most certainly it cannot be
  A native of our town;"
And he turned him round to his mamma,
  Who set her teacup down.

KG

But Dolly simply looked at them,
  She did not speak a word;
"She has no voice!" said Finikin;
  "It's really quite absurd."

Then Finikin's mamma observed,
  "Dear Prince, it seems to me,
She looks as if she'd like to drink
  A cup of my bohea."

So Finikin poured out her tea,
  And gave her currant-pie;
Then Finikin said, "Dear mamma,
  What a kind Prince am I!"

Heigh ho!—time creeps but slow;
I've looked up the hill so long;
None come this way, the sun sinks low,
And my shadow's very long.

They said I should sail in a little boat,
Up the stream, by the great white mill;
But I've waited all day, and none come my way,
I've waited—I'm waiting still.

They said I should see a fairy town,
With houses all of gold,
And silver people, and a gold church steeple;—
But it wasn't the truth they told.

My house is red—a little house,
　A happy child am I,
I laugh and play the livelong day
　I hardly ever cry.

I have a tree, a green, green tree,
　To shade me from the sun;
And under it I often sit,
　When all my work is done.

My little basket I will take,
　And trip into the town;
When next I'm there I'll buy some cake,
　And spend my bright half-crown.

THREE little girls were sitting on a rail,
    Sitting on a rail,
    Sitting on a rail;
Three little girls were sitting on a rail,
    On a fine hot day in September.

What did they talk about that fine day,
    That fine day,
    That fine day?
What did they talk about that fine day,
  That fine hot day in September?

The crows and the corn they talked about,
    Talked about,
    Talked about;
But nobody knows what was said by the crows,
  On that fine hot day in September.

Ring the bells—ring!
Hip, hurrah for the King!
The dunce fell into the pool, oh!
The dunce was going to school, oh!
The groom and the cook
Fished him out with a hook,
And he piped his eye like a fool, oh!